MW00445311

A Bible in Her Pocket

Written by Ashlie Gillit
Illustrated by Debbie Crump

The year was 1889. Twelve-year-old Helen Cadbury walked into the Mission Hall, already buzzing with activity. Volunteers rushed about caring for people who had come in from the poorest parts of Birmingham, England.

Helen noticed her father moving among them. Smartly dressed and well-to-do, he was co-owner of the Cadbury Chocolate Company. He had built this hall for the sole purpose of reaching out to the needy community of Birmingham.

Poor families received food and clothing in this little mission hall, but that was not all. The Gospel was freely preached to all who entered. In fact, on this Sunday night, they were holding a special Gospel meeting.

"The Gospel meeting is about to begin," Helen's father announced.

GOSPEL MEETING 7:30 TONIGHT

Helen gathered a few small children
and they all sat down
on the wooden benches.

Everyone sang hymns enthusiastically. Many of the volunteers had once been poor and needy themselves, slaves to drunkenness and gambling. But through the saving grace of Christ, they became changed people. They now worked tirelessly so others could hear the truth of God's Word.

The preacher's sermon was clear.
"Believe on the Lord Jesus Christ and thou shalt be saved."

Helen knew that her parents were faithful Christian people. Their lives were a constant testimony of God's love. She had often helped them in their mission work, but she knew that none of that made her a Christian.

"Is there anyone here today that would stand up and publicly proclaim the name of Jesus?" The preacher's question broke through her thoughts. Helen's heart burned within her. She knew what she must do. She stood up and walked to the small room at the back of the building. There she knelt and cried out to Jesus to forgive her and save her from her sins.

When she opened her eyes, the first thing she saw was the joyful face of her father. He was thrilled that she was now a child of God!

Helen wanted to share the Gospel with her friends at school.
But how could she make sure the girls knew that she was
sharing God's words and not her own?

"Oh," she thought, "I could bring my Bible to school and
keep it in my desk!"

Now she was ready to share God's own words whenever the
need arose.

She decided to begin by speaking to her friend Anna the next day.

"I became a Christian a few weeks ago!" said Helen.

"I'm a Christian as well. I go to church," answered Anna.

Helen replied, "I don't think going to church makes you a Christian. Will you read my Bible with me?"

The two girls read Helen's Bible together during break time. Anna went home thinking of all she had heard from her friend. She found a Bible at home and began reading it every night.

A few days later, Anna understood *she needed a Saviour.*

Helen and her Christian friends were bold about their faith. They invited everyone to read the Bible with them at school. Their Bible group began to grow.

The girls often missed good opportunities while they ran to get their Bibles from their desks. They decided to sew pockets on their school dresses and began to carry small New Testaments in them.

Now they could be ready to answer questions at a moment's notice!

HOLY BIBLE

POCKET TESTA

POCKET TESTAMENT LEAGUE

I HEREBY ACCEPT MEMBERSHIP IN THE POCKET TESTAMENT LEAGUE BY MAKING IT THE RULE OF MY LIFE TO READ AT LEAST ONE CHAPTER IN THE BIBLE A DAY, AND TO CARRY A BIBLE OR TESTAMENT WITH ME WHEREVER I GO.

Name: _____ Date: _____

Helen and the girls named their group, 'The Pocket Testament League.'

To join the league, you had to sign a pledge to:

✓ carry a New Testament with you
✓ read it every day
✓ use it to share the Gospel with others

Helen's father would give a New Testament to anyone who made that promise.

By the time Helen left school a few years later, *60 students had come to Christ!*

Time passed, and Helen grew up. She married a man named Charles Alexander, and together they traveled around the world sharing the Gospel. They also began a movement called... can you guess it? The Pocket Testament League!

What began as a small group of young girls carrying Bibles in their pockets turned into a worldwide movement that brought the Bible to thousands of people.

Helen said, *"If only we could get people to read the Book for themselves, it would surely lead them to Christ!"*

Helen had no idea that sharing her Bible with a friend would turn into a worldwide movement.

She simply obeyed God in the way she could, and God blessed her efforts!

What could God do with you, young Christian? Helen and her friends are no longer here, but you are!

Would you take up the same pledge these girls did?
Would you pledge to:

✓ carry your Bible with you
✓ read it every day
✓ use it to share the Gospel with others

"If only we could get people to read the Book for themselves, it would surely lead them to Christ!"

A Timeline of

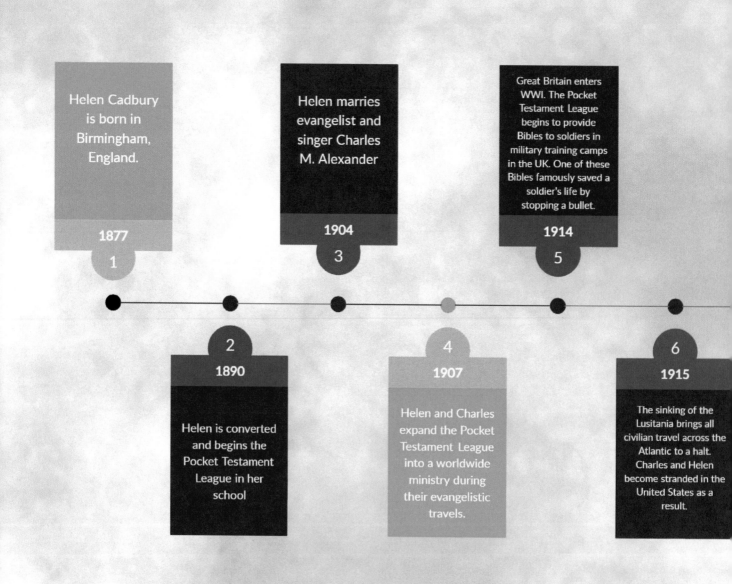

Helen Cadbury is born in Birmingham, England.

1877

1

2
1890

Helen is converted and begins the Pocket Testament League in her school

Helen marries evangelist and singer Charles M. Alexander

1904

3

4
1907

Helen and Charles expand the Pocket Testament League into a worldwide ministry during their evangelistic travels.

Great Britain enters WWI. The Pocket Testament League begins to provide Bibles to soldiers in military training camps in the UK. One of these Bibles famously saved a soldier's life by stopping a bullet.

1914

5

6
1915

The sinking of the Lusitania brings all civilian travel across the Atlantic to a halt. Charles and Helen become stranded in the United States as a result.

Helen Cadbury's Life

The United States enters WWI and the Pocket Testament League begins distributing Bibles to American soldiers as well.

1917

7

Charles Alexander dies. Helen continues the work with the Pocket Testament League on her own. She also begins writing her first book, a biography of her late husband.

1920

9

Helen dies at the ripe old age of 92. Until the day of her death, she never lost the healthy habit of carrying her pocket Testament with her everywhere she went.

1969

11

8

1918

After the end of the war, Charles and Helen return to England

10

1939

Helen is involved in efforts to help a large number of Jews escape Germany and Austria before the start of WWII.

Bibliography:

Helen Cadbury and Charles M Alexander by Simon Fox
A Romance of Song & Soul Winning by Helen C. Alexander
Pocket Testiment League Website https://www.ptl.org/

If you would like to have your own Bible please send an email to contact@cchtrust.org.uk and we will send you a Bible free of charge!

Made in the USA
Monee, IL
27 September 2023